To my Da[...]

Lots of lov[...]

An Unexpected Hero

An Unexpected Hero

L. P. Hansen

CreateBooks

www.createbooks.co.nz

First published by CreateBooks
Hamilton, New Zealand

Text © L. P. Hansen 2014

Illustrations © CreateBooks 2014

ISBN 978-0-9941102-7-5

Title: An Unexpected Hero
Author: L. P. Hansen
Publisher: CreateBooks NZ
Contact: www.createbooks.co.nz
info@createbooks.co.nz
Format: Paperback
Publication Date: 2014
ISBN: 978-0-9941102-7-5

Cover: Scott Pearson
Visual Evolutions.co.nz

For Rich and Mike

Chapter 1

Matt rummaged in his backpack, pretending to be looking for something so he could be the last one getting on the bus. It was his first morning at this country school, the same one his father had attended as a boy. Today of all days, the entire school was going on a trip to town, just his luck! He wasn't yet up to joining the other kids of his age jostling to get to the back of the bus. He still couldn't get over how small the school was. Year Eight had just two boys and three girls and with him, that made six kids in the class.

At his old school, his class year by itself filled

up a bus. Here the whole school fitted into one, with seats left over. And what a bus! Rather than the sleek city buses that Matt was used to, this one was so old, round and squat that it looked like a kid's toy. The driver was a woman. He could see her filling in a newspaper crossword puzzle as she waited.

'Hurry up, Matt,' urged the teacher beside him. She looked around, evidently waiting for someone else as well.

Matt zipped up his backpack and cautiously stepped on board. Mrs. Foster seemed okay. He noticed her jacket and bag on one of the front seats and took another front seat behind the driver. A moment later, a farm truck pulled to a halt and a fat, elderly man levered himself out from the passenger side. He stumped over to the bus, talking loudly to the waiting teacher.

Mrs. Foster welcomed him with obvious relief and ushered him onto the bus. To Matt's dismay, the man subsided into the seat beside him, greeting the driver gruffly.

As the bus set off, Matt looked out the window at the unfamiliar scenery. He jumped as the man beside him spoke.

'What's your name, lad?'

'Uh, Matt.'

'Matt who? Speak up! Not from round here, are you?' Matt wished he didn't have to talk so loud.

'I'm staying here with my grandparents until the end of term.'

The bushy white eyebrows lowered in a frown.

'Grandparents, eh? Lived here long, have they? Give me a name, boy.'

'Anne and Peter Turner.'

'What! You're Pete Turner's grandson? By crikey, you've got a nerve, coming on a trip to a war memorial. Damn cheek!' The sharp eyes narrowed angrily in the pudgy face and the man turned away, leaving Matt gaping at the back of his head.

What was all that about? Matt felt his face begin to flame but, remembering his promise to Mum, took a deep breath and kept silent.

After about twenty minutes trundling through farmland, the bus was stopped and parked in the two-lane road that seemed to be the main street of the town. Again Matt waited until last before getting off and joining the others around a tall stone war memorial set into a small patch of grass. Near the bus, an argument was going on between Mrs. Foster and the fat man. For some reason, Matt felt sure he was the cause of their disagreement. Eventually the old fellow turned away and crossed the road, disappearing into an RSA club.

'Good riddance to old Grumpy-guts. Bad luck having him sit with you,' came a cheerful voice beside him. Matt recognised him as Paul, one of the two Year Eight boys he'd been introduced to. The other one who he remembered as Ryan joined them. Thankfully they'd seemed friendly enough that morning.

'Yeah. He suddenly went all weird on me.'

'He's pickled in alcohol, that's what my dad

says,' Ryan laughed. 'He's the only old soldier left around here and he's always grumpy.'

Matt shrugged and grinned back. 'He's not too keen on my grandfather, by the sound of it.'

'Forget it. Hey, it's going to be great having another boy in our class; it evens things up a bit with the girls,' Ryan went on. 'Mrs. Foster said your dad used to go to this school?'

Matt nodded. 'Mine too. At least yours got away. Must be quite a shock being here after the big city.'

'It's okay,' Matt shrugged. 'Just different.'

Mrs. Foster was calling everyone to gather around the memorial. She seemed a bit flustered but determined to be cheerful. 'Now everyone, try and find some names you know on the memorial. Our guest will join us later,' she added, 'after he's finished his business.'

'Finished his beer, more likely,' someone muttered.

With a lot of good-natured shoving and

pushing, the kids clustered round the stone, competing to read the names carved on its sides. Matt could see that everyone except him soon found people they knew. There were no Turners on the lists and he felt a bit stupid staring at names that meant nothing to him.

Mrs. Foster came over to him. Matt had already gathered that they were here collecting background for a school project. Now she explained it was for a book to be called, 'Lest We Forget: Heroes From Our Past.' Each student would write a story to go in the book about a hero from their family. 'It doesn't have to be a war hero,' she explained, gesturing at the War Memorial. 'It can be a sporting hero or someone like that. You can also ask anyone in the district for help. Lots of families have lived round here for generations; the old people have long memories and some fine stories to tell.'

That sounded okay to Matt. He liked writing. 'How long have we got to do it?' he asked.

'The stories have to be finished in around three

weeks so they can be put together and made into a book by the end of term,' Mrs. Foster said. 'It's going to be professionally bound and presented to the community as a gift, on the last day of the school year.'

She smiled at Matt. 'That's a big event round here, a social evening that everyone looks forward to. People come even if they have no children at the school. Traditionally it's when Year Eight students give their farewell speech, before they go off to their colleges in the city. This year we've decided to let you six speak about the hero you've chosen. It'll make a nice change. Everyone stays for supper and then ...'

Matt was no longer listening. He looked away. A sick feeling had started up in his belly.

'Don't worry, Matt, I'm sure your grandparents will be able to help with this,' Mrs. Foster said kindly, as though she knew about his problem. But how could she? No one here knew, not even his Nan and Grandpa. Matt had made his parents promise that much, at least.

The old man arrived back and began raving on about ANZAC Day and 'our heroes, our boys who didn't come back.' Matt barely listened until he heard him snarl something about 'victory with no thanks to some people.' He looked up. The guy seemed to be glaring straight at him!

'Don't mind old Cedric, he's crazy,' Paul said in his ear. 'Sit with us on the way back.'

Matt was glad to join the noisy chattering group at the back of the bus. He tried to shake off the panic already gripping at his throat and forced himself ask, 'So who's he?' He jerked his head towards the front seat, whose occupant was already asleep and snoring.

'That's old Cedric, everyone calls him that. He's our local war hero,' offered one of the girls. 'He's over ninety and still lives in the same house where he was born.'

Matt tried to look impressed.

'His son still lives there too,' said another. 'That

was him in the truck back at school.'

'Imagine still living at home with your father when you're that old,' Paul added. 'Not that Freyberg could live anywhere else, most likely.'

'Freyberg?'

'Yeah, like that Governor General, the one with all the war medals. Who'd give their kid a name like that? '

'So was Freyberg a soldier too?' Matt asked. There was an awkward silence.

'Nah, he wouldn't be up for that. He's a bit – different. He looks after the house and helps on the farm, has done for years.' Ryan put in. 'His mother left when he was small so there's always been just the two of them.'

'Maybe that's why old Cedric's such a grumpy-guts!' someone giggled. The talk moved on.

'Hey Matt, I reckon you're the tallest kid in the school,' said a small girl with a shy grin. 'I saw you before; you beat Ryan by quite a bit. D'you play netball?' she added hopefully.' Will you play in my team?'

In the general laughter, Matt solemnly promised to try and learn. Everyone here seemed okay but he couldn't stop thinking about the school project. He wondered if he could fake being sick on the night of the speeches. Suppose they had to rehearse?

Walking home after school, he barely noticed his feet turning in at the long driveway and it wasn't until he heard the familiar voice that he realised where he was.

'Hey, wake up!' Grandpa called out cheerfully, stepping out from between the tall camellias that lined the driveway, pruning shears under his arm. 'You look as though you were having a nightmare.'

'Sorry,' Matt mumbled, avoiding looking at him.

'How was your first day?' Grandpa sounded concerned. 'Was school okay?'

'Sure,' Matt lied. 'Just getting used to it, that's all.'

Grandpa walked beside him to the house, his long legs matching Matt's stride. 'Nan's put out some cake for you. Then there's just time for a quick game of cricket before milking. Are you still keen to help at the shed again?'

Matt managed a smile. 'Sounds great.' He wouldn't think about the speeches just yet.

He enjoyed being around the cows, especially at milking time. Matt especially liked it that Grandpa's herd still had tails, not like the hideously tail-cropped creatures he'd seen in nearby paddocks. He'd quickly got wise to their lifted-tail warning, after being unceremoniously splashed during a visit to the shed a few days ago, when he'd first arrived at the farm.

His grandparents kept only a small number of cows. If it wasn't for the fact that they farmed organically, it wouldn't even be a viable herd. 'It used to be called old-fashioned, unscientific farming,' Grandpa joked. 'Now organics is the latest trend and we get top prices for our milk!'

Matt learned a bit more about dairying each time he visited the shed. Milking machinery had changed a lot over the years and his grandfather liked telling him about its history. In spite of all the systems he'd used during his fifty years as a farmer, he was particularly proud that he could still milk quickly by hand.

One thing that never changed was the shed clean-up and that was becoming Matt's job. With rubber boots and a high-pressure hose, it wasn't too bad and he guessed that every new shed-hand began with the cows' messes. After milking was over and after cleaning himself up and glancing at his emails, it was time for dinner.

What with answering Nan's questions about the kids at school and listening to Grandpa's tales about Dad's time there, Matt managed to avoid any mention of the book project. When the dishes were done and TV looked imminent, he decided to head for his room. 'Emails to write to Mum and Dad and some kids back home,' he explained. Anything to avoid thinking about the speeches.

As he powered up his laptop again, he wondered how to explain his first day at school to his city friends. It felt almost impossible, he thought. It was weird enough being in such a small school with all the kids in two classrooms. Having only two teachers who were married to each other was also peculiar. But it was more than that; it was the quiet self-contained feeling of the place, as though nothing beyond the district was necessary. Matt was wired into city buzz where something new and different was on offer, day and night.

Outside his window were only darkness and stars and tall shadowed trees. It was completely quiet apart from chirruping birds. Weren't they supposed to be asleep by now? He returned to his emails.

Chapter 2

The next day at school, most of the kids had already chosen a hero to write about and all seemed to be war heroes from their families. Matt listened amazed as girls as well as boys babbled on about battalions, squadrons, medals, battles and other military stuff. The main thing here was evidently to be handy with a gun or else be classed as a wimp. For Matt, this was a whole new way of looking at war!

He began to wonder why his parents never mentioned things like ANZAC parades, let alone went to them. Not that he wanted to, but they were a big deal around here.

When he got home after another long and confusing day, Grandpa was again waiting for him but this time there was no talk of cricket.

'A cup of tea and a chat,' he said, firmly directing Matt towards some fruit cake and scones set out on the kitchen table. 'Nan's at one of her meetings.'

'Paul's dad told me about your new school project,' he began at once, sitting down opposite Matt and pouring himself some tea. 'He thought you'd have mentioned it. Families are supposed to help with the stories and there isn't much time.'

Matt mumbled something about not getting around to it, but Grandpa went on as though he hadn't spoken.

'Has anyone at school been giving you a hard time?'

Matt was surprised. 'No, everyone's okay. Those I've met so far anyway.'

'So, you don't need any help, is that it? You've got your hero?'

'I don't have anyone to write about,' Matt said quickly, hoping to avoid his real reason for keeping quiet. 'Especially not a war hero. Mum and Dad and me, we never talk about war.'

Now it was Grandpa who looked surprised. 'Never?' he said, half choking on his tea.

Matt nodded. 'I've never been all that interested in guns and stuff. Me and my friends – we like other things. Maybe I'm a wimp,' he said, biting into a piece of cake.

Grandpa looked thoughtful. 'Wait here,' he said and fetched an old photo album from the living room.

'Suppose someone was trying to make you do something you thought was wrong,' he said as he sat down again and searched through the album pages. 'If you wouldn't do what they wanted, then suppose they tied you up, dragged you onto a ship and took all your clothes away?'

He ignored Matt's incredulous laugh and went on. 'Then they locked you in a cabin with no portholes and made you travel like that halfway round the world to England. Would you do what they wanted then?'

'It depends what it was,' Matt was cautious.

'If they wanted you to kill people?'

'Then they could keep me locked up, for all I cared!' Matt said.

'Then you, my boy, are no wimp. That's the spirit of our family.'

'So all that happened to one of your relations?' Matt asked, puzzled.

For answer, Grandpa pointed to a picture in the album of a man with a long, narrow face. The photo on the thick black paper was brown and faded, with spidery writing underneath and Matt squinted to read it.

'Archie?' he queried, looking up.

'Archibald Baxter. He was my mother's second cousin so he's a distant relation of yours too,' Grandpa said. 'That's what happened to him, a hundred years ago.'

'Was it terrorists who kidnapped him?'

'No, they were ordinary New Zealanders.'

Matt frowned. 'How come? Why did they want him to kill people?'

'It was wartime,' Grandpa explained. 'The time of World War One in Europe and Archie wouldn't get involved in it. He was what's called a pacifist, but in those days they called them conchies.'

'Conchies?' Matt queried.

'Means conscientious objectors. Archie didn't believe in war as a way of solving differences, so he wouldn't do any military work, obey orders, or even wear a uniform.'

'So that's why they took away his clothes?' Matt asked incredulously.

'Yes, they thought they'd be able to make him wear it if they did.' Grandpa sounded disgusted.

'That's sick!' Matt protested.

'Yes, it was sick. Archie's refusing to fight didn't mean he wasn't brave. He went up against the culture of the times and that takes guts.

'The Baxters were a big family. Almost all of his six brothers agreed with his beliefs. Some went to prison for refusing to join the war, although none went quite as far as Archie did. So would he be heroic enough for your school project?' Grandpa's voice sounded strange.

'That's quite a story, Grandpa. Maybe I could try and write about him but I'd need your help.'

His grandfather didn't answer straight away. It seemed like a long time until he came back from wherever his thoughts had taken him. 'Okay Matt, you can count on me,' he said finally. 'A lot of people round here have probably never heard of Archie Baxter or else they've forgotten about him. It's a story that'll raise a few eyebrows though.'

Matt felt awkward about asking more questions, although he wanted to. 'He looks nice,' he said instead, studying the photo.

'One day, you might read the book he wrote about those years during the war and then you'll understand that face,' Grandpa agreed, closing the album.

That night Matt couldn't sleep. This Archie Baxter did seem like someone he could use as his hero but that still left him stuck with his real problem. Somehow he had to get out of making that speech. But how?

Laying there, the memories he'd been trying to avoid surged back into his mind. He found himself replaying the speech days at his last school. It was like a horror movie. As Matt's turn to speak got closer and closer, no matter how hard he'd practised, he saw himself freeze rigid with fear. His jaw would clench, his throat close up, his mouth go dry and he'd be totally paralysed and mute. One year he'd even thrown up. If words did come out, his childhood stutter came back to ruin them.

By the time the ordeal was finally over, he'd be sick and sweating. Then everyone would tell him he'd get over it and not to worry, that it didn't matter. Liars, all of them. Because it did matter, and year after year it only got worse.

Matt found himself thrashing around at the

awful memories. The sheets and blankets felt hot and stifling and as he kicked them off, he remembered Archie Baxter having all his clothes taken away. Grandpa said he was made to march round the ship in his underwear. How gross was that? And all because he refused to wear a uniform? Yet he still didn't give in to their orders. Matt had to admit the guy was impressive, even if it sounded like an insane kind of courage.

He wondered if there was the faintest chance that some of that bravery could have trickled down into his own blood, kind of like DNA? He'd read about family traits and genetics. Archie was a relation, even if it was very distant.

It was strange to think of being in such a big family. Matt wondered what it would be like to have so many brothers. As an only child himself with parents who were also the only kids in their families, he couldn't even imagine it.

One reason he liked the room he was sleeping in was because it was full of family memories.

Some old-fashioned boys' adventure books were still on the shelves, with their faded covers and brown-spotted pages. There was a dusty rock collection, two ancient tennis racquets and boxes of junk that he hadn't investigated. Knowing that not only his father but Grandpa had grown up in this house helped him relax enough to fall asleep.

So the next day, when Mrs. Foster checked that everyone had found a hero to write about, Matt kept silent. Even if he didn't choose Archie Baxter, Mum might have some other suggestions, he told himself.

'Got a soldier somewhere in the family, have you?' Ryan asked idly. Matt was sitting between him and Paul in class.

'Not a soldier; an okay hero though.' Matt was noncommittal. 'You?'

'Some colonel cousin of my mum's, never heard of him before.' Ryan sighed. 'Boring.'

Matt smiled to himself. If he did tell Archie's story, it wouldn't be boring.

At lunchtime, he enjoyed tossing a ball around with the other two boys. They also showed him how to slip out of the school grounds and clamber down to a wide river. 'It's Senior Kids Only territory, always has been. Dad said it's where everyone used to come to smoke,' Paul explained.

'You?' Matt was curious.

'No way, smoking stinks! Girls don't like ashtray breath anyway.'

The three boys high-fived and then took turns swinging on a long knotted rope out over the clear, fast-moving water. For the first time since Mum had gone into hospital, Matt felt himself begin to really relax.

'So what's wrong with your Mum? Yesterday, Mr. Foster just said she wasn't well.' It was as though Paul had read his mind.

'She's having a baby. She lost one a while back and she could lose this baby too, so they've put her in hospital on bed rest.'

'Tough,' Ryan said and stopped.

Matt guessed he didn't want to ask any more, especially about dad. Lots of kids had fathers who didn't live at home.

'Dad's had to go to Hong Kong; big problems with his work,' he offered.

'What's he do?' Ryan sounded interested.

'He's in I.T. He's the only one who can sort out some major mess but it means he might be away for a couple of months'

'I.T. beats farming!' Ryan's tone was envious. 'Bet you miss them though.'

Matt nodded. 'Mum writes to me when she can, and they both email a bit. Dad's really busy though.'

There was silence.

'My hero's a colonel called Henry,' Ryan said, changing the subject. 'The cousins called him Horrible Henry. He ponced around North Africa and Egypt in 1940 giving orders and then kept it up when he got home, apparently. Who's yours going to be?'

Matt hesitated. 'I haven't decided.'

'I've found an airman,' Paul said. 'Angus, my great-aunt's boyfriend. He got killed in the Battle of Britain, World War Two.'

'After he'd dropped heaps of bombs on the bad guys, I hope?' Ryan grabbed the rope and started swinging out wildly.

Chapter 3

In class that afternoon, Matt couldn't concentrate. Even in class, all the kids seemed to mostly talk about rugby, farming and what was on TV. He couldn't care less about rugby or farming and hardly ever bothered with TV, but to these kids, this was normal. Now that war was the new favourite topic, Matt still had nothing to add to the general chat.

He missed talking to his friends about ordinary things, like computers, skateboards or messing about with his telescope. He'd set the telescope up on the back porch as soon as he arrived. That was one good thing about being in the country; the night sky was clear without the city lights. Maybe he'd see if Ryan or Paul wanted to come over one night and check it out. He'd wait for a bit though, until living with his grandparents didn't feel so strange.

The summer term was already part way over and Matt knew he had to make it through only six more weeks of school before the holidays started. His parents had discussed this endlessly with him, after Dad decided to go to Hong Kong.

Mum's hospital bed rest was already scheduled when Dad's work problems erupted and it had been a difficult decision for him to make. Fixing the computer chaos and re-training local staff would take him out of the country for around six weeks, he reckoned. The bonus was that it would guarantee him at least two months off over the summer to spend with Matt and Mum, and the new baby, of course.

Matt had jumped at the chance to spend time on the farm with Dad's parents. They'd often come to stay over the winter, when the cows were 'drying off' from milking and he felt comfortable with them. When he was younger, Matt had once spent Christmas with them and enjoyed that too, although it had been different with Mum and Dad there. They were happy to have him to stay and everyone eventually agreed it would be the best solution.

Thinking about helping with the cows had felt good but Matt hadn't thought much about school. Dad had said it was a great little place, but he was used to it.

Matt walked home slowly and found Grandpa fixing something in the tractor shed. Tools were piled up on the battered surface of the big old work bench and Matt could see it was years since anyone had hung them up against the matching outlines penciled on the wall. He wondered who'd drawn all those outlines. His father perhaps? Grandpa himself?

On an impulse, he perched on a wooden saw horse and started to tell his grandfather about his encounter the previous day with the old soldier. 'What did he mean about me having a cheek going on that school trip?' he asked cautiously.

'Ah, Grumpy-guts Cedric.' Grandpa put aside his work and sat down heavily. 'Anything to do with war gets him steamed up, Matt. I might look old, but I remember old Cedric being grumpy when I was your age. It's the way he's always lived, it's a wonder it hasn't killed him.'

'What d'you mean? I thought he was the great war hero around here?' Matt was puzzled.

'You're right, he is that too. It's quite a story, d'you want to hear it?

Matt nodded.

'Cedric's dad was a soldier, too, in the First World War. He pulled some strings when the second one started so that Cedric could join up when he was only 17, I think. After four years, he was invalided back from Europe, barely 21 years old and already a hero, after fighting in several campaigns. He recovered quickly, he was young and fit and apparently spent the last part of the war campaigning against the 'conchies', just like his father.'

'I don't get it?' Matt frowned.

'Old Cedric had been brought up to detest pacifists. His father has taught him it was okay to go out of his way to publicly rubbish them and their families, label them traitors and cowards, and make trouble for them whenever he could.'

Grandpa sighed and rubbed his eyes. 'Lots of people listened to Cedric because they'd listened to his father. Also he was the young war hero, and very persuasive. He would do things like lobby sports groups and other organisations to ban membership to pacifists' families the way they did in his father's time. In those days, one kid was even refused the top prize in his school because of his father's beliefs. In a district like this where everyone knows everyone else's business, someone like Cedric can cause a heap of trouble.'

'Sounds like a real stirrer,' Matt said.

'Some people thrive on having a cause that makes them look good. Pacifists can seem like easy targets too, because they won't fight back. The committed ones are willing to tough it out, but it can be hard on their wives and kids when shopkeepers won't serve them and people ignore them or put white feathers in their letter boxes.' He gave a wry chuckle at Matt's puzzled expression.

'It's a sign for cowardice.'

'A feather!' Matt laughed. 'Big deal. You said your mother was a relation of the Baxters, so did he make trouble for you?'

'It was a distant connection. No, Cedric never bothered us directly. My mother was very committed to pacifism and loyal to her family tradition, but she wasn't one to preach about it. You never knew her but you'd have liked her, Matt. She and my father managed to always be civil to Cedric, even if they didn't have much time for his shenanigans.'

Grandpa pushed back his sparse white hair.

'I've had my share of disagreements with the old fellow, lots of people have, but I may need to remind him it's me he's got to reckon with. I won't have him upsetting you!'

'I'm okay, Grandpa,' Matt said hastily. 'It was nothing. The kids at school said he's always grumpy about something. I'm just glad you've told me about him. His problems are nothing to do with me or you, by the sound of it.'

Grandpa nodded. 'If you're sure. He's harmless these days. I've heard he's grumpy because he can't sleep; maybe it's to do with what he did when he was in uniform all those years ago.'

He rubbed his cheek reflectively. 'Well, Matt, you've got me remembering things I haven't thought about in years. This Hero project is going to stir up all sorts of memories for people. Has this put you off writing about Archie?'

'I'm still deciding.' Matt didn't want to admit that he was getting curious about pacifists. What was it about them that got people so steamed up?

Chapter 4

Arriving early at school the next morning, Matt found Paul and Ryan waiting for him. Without a word, they jerked their heads towards the hedge and Matt followed them down to the river.

'Surprise!' The three girls from their class were already sitting in the long grass with a large plastic container between them. 'It's Pancake Day!' one of them said, smiling at him. 'A Year Eight tradition. We decided every Thursday would be Pancake Day, as long as it's sunny.'

Matt beamed back. This was Susan, small and lively with short brown hair and a really neat figure.

'You guys bring the maple syrup and orange

juice and we take turns at bringing the pancakes!' offered Shelley, the leggy blonde with the light blue eyes. 'We thought we'd let you off today, since this is your first week.'

Shelley seemed okay yet Matt felt uncomfortable around her. She reminded him of someone but he couldn't think who it was.

'So how d'you like it here?' asked the third girl, Bronwyn, as she passed Matt a thick pancake, slathered in syrup.

'It's getting better by the day,' he answered, eating it quickly before the syrup trickled down onto his shirt. 'Is this really a tradition?'

'It is now,' Ryan said, his mouth full of food. 'A few months back, we figured that since we can't go to McD's on the way to school for a pancake breakfast like you city kids, we'd make our own.'

'This is heaps better than McD's,' Matt said, leaning back in the bracken and looking up at the tree ferns arching overhead. 'That's a sad place in the morning, full of lonely people and too many hungry kids buying breakfast. This is brilliant!'

The six of them chatted about nothing in particular until the school bell rang. Matt wondered if there were any particularly close friendships going on but couldn't be sure.

They rinsed their sticky hands and cups in the river while Susan packed up the remains in her backpack. 'Your turn for the pancakes next week,' she reminded Shelley 'We need some more maple syrup too, guys.'

That breakfast was Matt's introduction to what he came to think of as the Year Eight family. During the days that followed, he realised that the five kids had known each other all their lives and knew each other's families equally well. They knew his grandparents too. In class, they cooperated readily and without fuss, which was just as well as their year frequently worked unsupervised.

Matt wasn't used to being trusted with so much independence but liked it. He also enjoyed the way the others included him in everything and even found himself practising rugby passes one lunchtime. Just as well, as sports practice often meant either rugby or netball, girls and boys playing together.

With the end of term approaching, there were tests to revise for and assignments to finish. The teachers allowed very little time during the day to talk about the Hero project. They checked that no one was having difficulties and then left it to the families to supervise the writing of the stories at home.

This wasn't unusual, Matt gathered. He'd wondered how to bring up the subject but needn't have worried. Nan mentioned it the day after the pancake breakfast.

'Everyone at my yoga class today was talking about the school book,' she'd said, handing Grandpa a mug of tea after dinner. 'Even the five year olds are writing Hero stories, I hear. You're thinking of choosing Archie Baxter, Matt?'

'Maybe, I haven't decided. Mum and Dad are

both from such small families; I don't know of anyone else to write about. Mum's got no relations that I know much about. Maybe Dad's got some cousins on your side?' he asked his grandmother hopefully.

'We're a small family too,' Nan answered. 'I can't think of anyone else where enough's known to write a story about them. As for Archie, you must make up your own mind, Matt. People like him caused quite a stir in this district years ago, I've heard.'

She smiled mischievously at Matt. 'Before your Grandpa proposed to me years ago, he told me what it was like for him being a pacifist in a district where so many families have lost men to war. He wanted to make sure I knew what I was up for, moving here.'

She tossed her grey curls at the memory. 'I said that, being Irish, I could stand up for myself! Also I happen to agree with conscientious objectors. Irish women and children have always been left alone while their men went off to fight in one war after another. Even when they're home, they'd still fight each other, to keep in practice, as it were. And d'you know what used to rile me the most about it?' Her eyes flashed behind her glasses as she looked at Matt.

He shook his head, laughing.

'Those mad fellas come back from their wars all battered and bruised, missing bits of themselves and go straight into the pub. They drink themselves silly and sing self-pitying, sentimental songs all about themselves. Not a thought for their long-suffering families, left alone to manage. That's why I married this man.' She patted Grandpa's tanned and wrinkled hand.

'I'm still a Celt though,' Grandpa teased.

'A Celt with some Scottish sense, I'm happy to say.'

Matt couldn't help smiling at the pair of them. 'So were people mean to you two about pacifism? Like with white feathers and stuff? Grandpa told me about them.'

'They wouldn't dare!' Nan flared. 'But yes, there's deep feeling here about war. Anger too at the terrible losses. Some soldiers feel guilty at what they've done, and for surviving. Guilty people look for someone to blame.'

'In Archie's day, this country was tougher on its pacifists than most other nations,' Grandpa added. 'The government practically encouraged people to be hard on them. Mind you, one of our later Prime Ministers was so against military conscription he spent a year in prison for sedition! Peter Fraser, he was locked up in 1916, but that was nothing compared to what the military did to the 'conchies'.'

Nan nudged him. 'Maybe that's enough, Pete –'

'It's okay, Nan,' Matt said. 'I'd like to know what happened to Archie. I heard a bit about his trip to England, that's all.'

'It's a terrible story, Matt. Are you sure?' Nan looked doubtful.

'I'm sure. If I'm going to write about him, I either learn this stuff from you two or I read his book.'

'Okay then, here goes. I'll fill out what you've heard already,' Grandpa looked at the ceiling and then at Matt. 'Tell me when you've had enough and I'll stop.' He cleared his throat and began.

'There were thousands of Kiwi conscientious objectors, and to show the government meant business, fourteen of the best-known, including Archie and two of his brothers, were forced onto the troopship Waitemata and sent overseas, as I told you before.

'Before they left, they'd already faced enormous abuse aimed at breaking their spirit so they'd obey military orders. But they didn't want to be soldiers so they couldn't and they wouldn't.

'Archie was eventually sent to a terrible place they called Mud Farm in the western part of Belgium where he was tied to a post out in the open, hands strapped behind his back, feet roped up off the ground and left to hang like a dead man for hours, every day. Sometimes another man was tied alongside him.'

Matt could hardly believe what he was hearing. Grandpa's voice was strained and his knuckles showed white against his mug of tea.

'It was the Kiwi version of Field Punishment Number One, tougher than the toughest military punishment there is, Matt. They called it the Crucifixion. No matter whether it was snowing, raining or blazing hot, he was tied up like that every day, given no food or water, and often beaten afterwards. It went on for sometimes for weeks in a row. The men were barely conscious when they were cut down.' Grandpa coughed awkwardly.

'Did Archie die?' Matt heard his own voice sounding shaky.

'No, somehow he survived, and he still refused to follow military orders.'

Matt was incredulous. 'Surely they let him go home after that?'

'No, Matt, they were even more determined to break him. I think they were a bit afraid of him by then. So next they dragged him out to a battle front where the worst fighting was going on, certain he'd beg for a gun to defend himself.'

'Did he?' Matt had to ask, although he already guessed the answer.

'No. He said it turned him off war even more, if that was possible. During a bombardment, almost all of his company was killed and he was found half-dead and taken to a French hospital. He was in bad shape with memory loss and other problems. To cut a long story short, eventually he was shipped back to New Zealand.

'So he survived all that? He must have been incredibly tough.'

'Yes,' Grandpa smiled. 'An inspiring character. He must have been damaged but he lived on until he was 88. He had a very full life.'

'He deserved to,' Matt shivered. 'It's hard to believe people could be so mean to someone they knew, just because they wouldn't fight.'

'Yes,' Grandpa agreed. 'Some officers just couldn't understand that Archie would never support war, no matter what they did. That takes courage.

'It's time for our Scrabble game.' Nan's voice was firm. Matt leapt up gratefully to fetch the battered old box. He set out the game on the table and Freddy, the big farm cat, jumped onto a chair and leaned forward, whiskers quivering as he studied the board intently.

'He's planning his first move,' Nan said lightly, reaching to smooth his fur. 'He never misses a game.'

Neither did his grandparents. Matt knew how they relished their nightly Scrabble game. Each tried to outdo the other with carefully placed obscure words, so they could add to the legendary scores that were recorded in a special notebook. Matt remembered Dad talking about that notebook and the scores that went back over years. He joined in the game and managed to place 'oxen' on a triple word score, earning an approving grunt from Grandpa.

Later as she looked in at his bedroom to say good night, Nan lingered in the doorway. 'I don't want you having nightmares,' she said. 'There's something important you should know about Archie. During the war, many of the ordinary soldiers liked him, even if they didn't understand him. He was a decent man and they felt bad about what was being done to him. They took real risks, giving him their chocolate rations, offering small kindnesses when they could. He wrote about that in his book, he was very grateful.' She wiped her glasses which were rapidly misting up.

'You needn't feel sorry for him, Matt. What he did was a free choice. Some of the more humane officers used to offer him war work away from the battlefields, instead of his punishments, but he refused because to him it would mean giving in to the world of war. He just tried to understand and to keep caring about humanity. To me, that's real courage.'

Matt felt a lump in his throat. 'Thanks, Nan.

That's good to hear.'

Yet as soon as she left, Matt felt his old fears invade him and he lay staring at the high ceiling with its white plaster mouldings and fly-speckled light shade. Okay, so Archie was brave, no doubt about that. But was he?

It was going to be hard enough being the stuttering idiot trying to give a speech. But if he'd written about someone who refused to join a war, while the others chose relations who'd fought and probably been killed, would his new friends see him as a coward as well?

Heck, it was a hundred years ago, surely people had forgotten. Maybe not old Cedric. But probably everyone else. Yet how could he be sure? There was no way of knowing.

What was Archie Baxter to him anyway? How come Dad never mentioned him, or any of this family tradition of pacifism?

Matt really wanted his time at Dad's old school to be okay. Dad had asked him not to do anything that would worry Mum. Any extra stress could make her lose the baby, the doctors had said. Then Mum had made him promise not to worry Nan and Grandpa, because they were getting old. What did they think he was? A trouble-making machine? And if he wasn't allowed to talk to anyone, who was there to help with his worries?

'Me,' he decided. 'There's no one else, so I have to take care of myself. It's just that I don't know what to do.' He went over his options for a long while before falling into an uneasy sleep.

Chapter 5

As soon as he woke the next morning, Matt knew that his confusion had sorted itself out as he slept. He stretched, almost dislodging Freddy who had jumped on his bed during the night and was curled up against him. 'Relax, big cat,' he said, scratching the stripey head. 'It's Saturday. No school.' As the rhythmic purr started up again, Matt lay there a moment, smoothing the tabby's thick fur.

Later, after he'd dressed and made himself some toast, he walked over to the shed to see how Grandpa was going with the morning milking. Freddy prowled along beside him, tail erect. The herd was ambling out of the yard as they got there,

Matt got going on his usual tasks and whistled to the birds darting round the yard as he pushed the stiff broom vigorously along the wet concrete. The warm, sweet smell of the cows was still everywhere and he no longer cared about the messes they made.

'You're very cheerful this morning! You must have slept well. I didn't,' Grandpa yawned, scratching his head under his milking cap. 'All that talk about Archie stirred me up.'

'Me too. But I must have made my mind up after I finally went to sleep. I am going to write about him. Only because pacifism wasn't too popular round here, I want to keep quiet about it, for now. Will you still help me?'

'Well, yes, if you're sure. Meet me in the office after lunch around two, after I've had my afternoon nap and we'll sort out some papers,' Grandpa promised.

After lunch, Matt helped Nan in the vegetable garden while Grandpa supposedly 'put his feet up.'

As they tied up beans and weeded carrots, Freddy crouched between two rows of mounded-up potatoes, clearly wanting to play. Matt finally took pity on him and dangled some grass stems for the crazy cat to leap at.

'Off you go, Matt,' Nan said, laughing at their antics. 'Have a rest yourself, your grandfather's probably still asleep.

Yet when Matt looked into the office, he found his grandfather already hard at work. 'I couldn't rest, thinking about how much work there is to do,' he said. 'I wanted to make a start and get everything ready for you; dates, places, facts and figures. I've been planning to write a family history for a while and I know that you need lots of details.'

Matt looked with dismay at the piles of books and photo albums, surrounded by brimming boxes of papers. 'Concentrate,' he said to himself. 'Don't think about the speech, concentrate on the story.' So he tried to follow the complicated time line of Archie's life that his grandfather was creating. Several large sheets of paper had been stapled together and headed up with dates and place names. Under these headings, Grandpa was copying out extracts from Archie's book, 'We Will Not Cease.' Matt had started reading bits of it a few days ago.

He watched his grandfather uneasily for a while and then burst out, 'It's great what you're doing, Grandpa, but this is way too much stuff for me to use. It isn't supposed to be a story about Archie's whole life, remember? '

Grandpa concentrated on copying out a date without answering. His expression had set into what Matt had heard Nan call his Neolithic look.

Matt felt a rising panic. 'It's supposed to be a short story, Grandpa,' he said. 'Not a whole biography! I was hoping to keep it to just a dozen paragraphs, put in some photos with captions, and keep the details to a minimum.'

Grandpa focused on the piece he was copying out, still saying nothing.

'There'll be so many other stories in the book; I want ours to stand out. I planned to start with an attention-grabber to get people interested, make them want to read it. I'm not sure that facts and figures will do it.' Matt heard his voice starting to sound desperate.

Grandpa carefully underlined a heading, the disappointment clear on his face.

'We could make a scrapbook later with everything you've got here, Grandpa, use your timeline, keep all this information together. It won't be wasted.'

'Now, that's a fine idea!' Grandpa looked up at last. 'Nan could help with her computer!'

Nan's new computer was a joke between them. Grandpa had told Matt that since she'd started going to Senior Net classes, Nan never stopped talking about all the things she could do with her new fella, her Mac.

'So what shall we start with?' The tension had passed and Matt was keen to begin. Remembering some words from Archie's book, an idea was already forming.

They stared at the stapled pages until Matt said, 'Suppose I start it like a mystery, set the scene with clues and hold back on the names and facts? That should make the readers curious.'

He began to scribble rapidly. Reading over his shoulder, Grandpa made worried noises and shook his head. 'Nothing like any school project I've ever heard of,' he said.

However Matt soon had a paragraph he was pleased with. 'It's like the opening of a best seller,' Grandpa sounded uneasy.

'Read this, Nan,' said Matt, as they took it to the kitchen. 'It's the start of my Archie story. Just imagine you don't know who it's about.'

Nan read it aloud.

'The wrenching agony of his arms tied tightly behind him threatened to break the man's concentration but he refused to look away from the sky reflected in the muddy puddle at his feet.

Nor would he heed the pain of his knees and feet lashed to the post, leaving him sagging like a dead man. The stench of slime and filth mixed with the smell of his own fear as he hung there. 'Not much longer now,' he told himself. 'Only three more hours of this.' Then would come the beatings and only much later, merciful sleep. Yet again, he would try to bear it without complaint; try to survive for one more day. He could not, he would not give in.'

'Oh Matt,' she said, sitting down abruptly. 'That's so awful. I mean, it's awfully good. A fine start.'

'So you'd want to go on reading?'

Nan nodded.

'I need to get people wanting to know more about this mystery man and why he's being tortured.' Matt explained. 'Using Archie's name might put some of the locals off right away, from what you say.'

'I like the way he starts out as brave,' Nan said. 'That catches my interest right away.'

'See, nothing to worry about!' Matt said, grinning at his grandfather. 'If this is going to work, he has to be a surprise though, so don't tell anyone. Is it okay if I keep working in your office, Grandpa? I can help you with the scrapbook later.'

He returned to their papers and looked again at what he had written. He was going to tell this story and tell it his way. Surely once people knew what Archie was really like, they'd understand?

Matt kept writing all that afternoon. He read and wrote and then found himself cutting out most of what he'd written. He felt driven to give just the bare bones of Archie's story, with no padding to distract the reader.

'You look like you're about to explode,' Nan said, bringing him a late sandwich. 'In a good way, as though you've found your own way up a mountain and nothing's going to stop you.'

'The more I read about this guy, the more I feel he's a hero, even if others say he was a traitor. He deserves to be seen for what he truly is; I don't want to get into explaining him, trying to make him acceptable.' Matt said. 'D'you get what I'm trying to say?'

Nan sat down, listening closely.

'He lived what he believed in, didn't just talk about it, even though it must have been hard and lonely. He can't have cared what other people thought either, or he could never have done what he did,' Matt went on. 'I am what I am too, even if I fall to pieces on speech night, as I probably will. When I see what he was willing to go through, how can I worry about my problems?'

Nan raised a quizzical eyebrow then and he found himself blurting out his fears.

Later Matt marveled at how life could shove you into what felt like your worst nightmare and then pick you up and spit you out into the very place you needed to be. As he poured out his story, he'd virtually forgotten about Nan's amateur dramatics. Matt only vaguely remembered his father mentioning it but he soon learned that acting was her life-long passion. When it came to the human voice, his grandmother had years of experience in helping people just as scared as him. She'd apparently produced, directed and acted in countless plays that had won drama competitions not only in country districts but in the city

'I can help you as much or as little as you want,' Nan told him, matter-of-factly. 'I've a whole bag full of tricks to help people get past stage fright, plus other ways to work with managing the voice. You can try them all and use only what you need, whatever suits you best. After that, Matt, it's really over to you. And the cows, of course.'

It was then that she confided her secret to him. It turned out that years ago, she'd started practising her lines in front of the cows and found them to be the perfect audience. No matter how often she repeated her words, they listened patiently, interested and alert to the slightest change in her voice. 'I'd sometimes try a different way of saying a single word and I could swear their expressions changed. Or they'd look away and I'd just know it hadn't worked.'

Matt couldn't help laughing as he pictured the scene.

'Does Grandpa know?' he couldn't resist asking.

'If he does, he knows better than to mention it,' she said, making a throat-cutting gesture. 'And the same goes for you, Matt. You want me to keep your secret? You keep mine. Promise?'

'Promise.' Matt was already feeling stirrings of hope. Maybe he could do this thing after all.

They arranged to meet at a time when Grandpa was busy on the farm and Matt went back to his writing.

During the following days, Matt kept up his pattern of writing and cutting when he could, but now he passed on all his surplus pieces about Archie to Grandpa who was starting his scrapbook.

Together, they went through the stack of photo albums and eventually found a photo that showed Archie with some other men in detention camp and another taken after the war of him with his wife Millicent and their sons, Terence and James. The boys looked so serious, Matt thought, the younger kid showing no sign of the wild poet he was to become.

Chapter 6

Apart from the first evening when he'd set up his telescope, Matt had barely looked through it. There never seemed to be enough time. Also when he'd mentioned it to Paul and Ryan, they'd seemed puzzled that anyone would be interested in looking around a dark sky.

'What's there to see at night?' Paul asked. 'Just a few planes with lots of lucky people heading overseas.'

Matt decided not to try and explain, although from long habit, every evening he glanced up at the sky to see what the cloud cover was like.

He'd almost abandoned the idea of shared star

gazing when Susan called in with her mother one Sunday afternoon with some trays of vegetable seedlings for Nan. They were on their way home from the Farmers' Market, she explained to Matt, as she helped him carry the plants out to the garden. On the way back, she spotted the telescope on the verandah and stopped to look.

'Dad's taught all us kids about the stars,' she said, studying it with interest. 'He's taken us to the planetarium in the city a couple of times. He was a navigator on cargo boats before he met Mum. What can you see?'

Matt explained it was a basic 70 mm refractor scope. 'It's not the world's greatest,' he admitted 'but on a clear night you can see some good stuff. Especially here without the city lights. You could come over and try it some time,' he added.

'I'd like to.' Susan's smile was so warm that Matt forgot about the ripped shorts he was wearing and the t-shirt stained with green dribble from an over-affectionate cow.

During the days that followed, she'd joined him twice on evenings when the sky was clear. Matt could hardly believe his luck. Susan was great company. Also, she said nothing about the Hero project and he was grateful.

Matt enjoyed showing her what he knew and hearing about what she'd learned from her father. She was deft and quick with changing the telescope's eyepiece and lenses and they were relaxed and easy together.

How he loved to gaze at the southern constellations with her, and at the graceful arc of the Milky Way, flecked with its dozens of silver-white star clusters.

Although he kept quiet about their shared star gazing, someone had obviously found out. One morning an annoying little kid drew a huge heart in the dirt at school with Matt's and Susan's initials in it, and started going on about Matt's girlfriend.

Matt's embarrassment abruptly faded as Ryan stepped forward, his face hard. Without a word, he kicked away the offending symbol and strode off to join Paul.

At lunchtime, for the first time the two boys didn't look for Matt to join them at the river and he began to feel uneasy. Ryan was clearly the school leader, his rugby skills were undisputed and Matt was no threat to him there. But that the other boy liked Susan –Matt hadn't bargained on that.

The day got worse. That afternoon, Matt was asked to read some stupid poem to the whole room. As he stood up, already nervous, his traitorous voice chose that moment to betray him.

It was ages since he'd blocked so badly, yet faced with an uncomprehending sea of faces, Matt forgot everything he'd been taught about managing his stutter. 'The b-boats b-bobbed b-bravely on the b-blue sea,' he heard himself blurt out, and blushed crimson with shame.

Everyone was staring at him, including Mr. Foster. Understanding finally, the teacher said briskly, 'Thank you, Matt. Bronwyn, will you carry on?'

But the damage was done. Matt sank into his seat, not daring to look at anyone. He breathed deeply, trying to relax, but it was hopeless.

Matt's stuttering, or blocking as he'd learned to call it, had started when he was very young and been sent to stay with relatives. That whole family had a mean streak, Matt knew that now.

Once again, his mother's pregnancy had led to the separation. Her 'cranky cervix' as she called it, had allowed their unborn baby out into the world, far too young to survive. Matt's father, unable to care for his distraught wife as well as his small son, had been grateful for a distant cousin's offer to take Matt for a few weeks.

The family had a way of putting people down and found Matt's childish efforts at speaking hilarious. Matt soon learned that if he said anything wrong, he would be mimicked and made fun of. He also shared the bedroom of a boy a few years older, a swaggering bully, even then.

Every night his cousin told him stories about

his parents not wanting him, saying that's why he'd been sent away and Matt began to live in terror that it was true.

Although it was so many years ago, he could still remember the miracle of his father's unexpected visit and his own instant removal. He'd not seen that family since, yet although he'd been taken home and showered with love and reassurance, it was years until he could overcome the habit of 'blocking' on certain words.

'This Hero project's getting to me,' he realised. Ryan's sudden rage had also unsettled him.

It was then that he heard the soft whisper, followed by sniggers. 'B-Bronwyn, pass me the b-book, will you?'

Shelley had mimicked him perfectly, too quietly for Mr. Foster to hear. That was it! With her pale hair and cold blue eyes, Shelley reminded him of the girl in that family, his mean cousin.

Matt remembered her with a shudder. A

helpless fury rose up in his chest and he turned away. He had little doubt about what lay ahead for him now.

.

Chapter 7

Matt eventually found himself at almost the end of writing Archie's story. It was going okay but he still felt unsatisfied.

'I don't know how to finish it,' he said to Nan. 'It seems such a waste, everything that Archie and the others went through. No one takes any notice of their ideas any more. All over the world, it's still wars and more wars, governments everywhere getting people to fight and kill each other for some dumb cause.'

'Not quite everywhere!' Nan gave him a knowing look. 'I might know just what to end with. You'll have to do a computer search to get the details, but I can give you a clue.' She whispered something into his ear and returned to her baking. She was making sourdough bread, Matt's favourite.

Half an hour later, Matt burst excitedly into the kitchen. 'Hey, Nan, you're a genius! How did you know?'

Nan laughed. 'You should know by now that country women don't just sit around knitting!'

Soon Matt was able to add his completed story to the growing pile on the Mr. Foster's desk, just in time to meet the deadline. On the title page, he'd called it 'An Unexpected Hero' and made sure that neither Archie's name nor the words New Zealand appeared until near the end of the story, to keep the suspense going for the reader.

It was a bit like a thriller, Matt knew and he was pleased with it. Researching and writing Archie's story had been about the only thing going okay for him lately.

'This looks very professional, Matt,' Mr. Foster said, looking at the neat columns of well-spaced type, the generous paragraphing and captioned photos. 'I've no time to read it now but I can see you've got good computer skills. Those wide margins will be a great help when the book gets put together.'

'Nan helped me with the layout,' Matt suppressed a smile at the memory. 'And Grandpa helped with the research.'

'Just add your full name and the name of your hero to this list here. We've asked someone to create a contents page and index for us; he needs all the information today.'

Matt hesitated so long over the notebook that Mr. Foster became impatient. 'Just write the names down, Matt, I don't have all day.'

'It's just that I'd hoped to keep my hero's name a surprise,' Matt tried his best to look innocent.

'Surprise us on the night then, will you? Hurry up, Matt, there's a lot to do before all this goes away to the book binders.'

Reluctantly Matt scribbled down his name

followed by Archie's. He turned the page and folded it back, leaving a fresh page ready for the next entry, although probably no one would recognise Archie's name, he reasoned.

He was wrong.

When he arrived at school after the weekend, instead of ignoring him as they'd mostly done since the heart in the dirt incident, Ryan and Paul were waiting for him. Ryan's handsome face was dark and surly and Paul stood behind him, looking a bit shifty.

'Your family hero's a conchie? Archibald Baxter?' Ryan pronounced the name as though it was poisonous. It was hardly a question and Matt said nothing.

'We've been hearing bad stuff about him,' Ryan went on, his eyes narrowing. 'He made everyone else do the dangerous work, real soldiers who got killed because of him. Anyone who likes 'conchies' isn't welcome round here.'

'Conchies are pathetic, won't even help

protect their own people. Can't you find a real hero anywhere in your family?' Paul sounded incredulous.

Matt felt the blood rush to his face and his chin went up. 'You d-don't know anything. Archie B-baxter was a hero, you'll s-see!' he managed to blurt out angrily as he walked away. His legs were shaking but he forced himself to cross to the other side of the playground where an impromptu soccer game was going on.

'I hate this school,' he thought, kicking the grass. 'I hate this stupid project and I hate being here.'

During morning games, Ryan expertly tripped him twice, and both he and Paul grinned as Matt crashed to the ground, grazing first an elbow and then a knee. 'S-sorry, M-matt,' they chorused. It was their regular jibe these days. They seemed to think it was hilarious, but this time Ryan sneered, 'C-cowardly c-conchie.'

'Lift your feet, Matt,' Mr. Foster called from

the sideline, where he'd been unable to see what happened. 'You'll be no use to a team if you keep tripping over them!'

Matt was still white-hot with rage when regular classes resumed. He ignored the boys beside him and refused to react when, at lunchtime, they disappeared down to the river without him. 'No self-pity,' he ordered himself.

He was helping some of the juniors try out some skateboard stunts when he saw Susan, Bronwyn and Shelley watching him. They smiled when they noticed him looking and he turned abruptly back to the little kids. Girls' sympathy was all he needed, he thought with disgust. No doubt they'd already heard about his 'p-pathetic p-pacifist.'

Shelley was really getting to him lately. She kept finding him on his own and asking him odd questions. Matt was certain she was up to something and avoided her as much as he could.

In question time that afternoon, she asked in an innocent tone, 'Mr. Foster, what would you say is the definition of heroism? I was thinking it's people who risk their lives for others.' Matt was sure she gave deliberate weight to the word, 'others'.

'A fair answer, Shelley.'

Matt couldn't miss her triumphant smirk.

'Heroism involves putting others first, even at your own risk.' Mr. Foster went on. 'It's the spirit that lets someone face danger or pain without showing fear.'

'Even though that p-person might still be afraid?' Matt couldn't help himself.

'Yes, Matt, an excellent point.' Mr. Foster was pleased. 'Courage in the face of fear is probably the greatest heroism of all.'

Matt leaned back, satisfied. Archie knew all about fear but he didn't give in to it, and his efforts were for others, whether they knew it or not.

He didn't look at Shelley but knew that if there was more trouble coming, he'd face it head on. There'd been too many times in his life when hiding from trouble was all Matt had been able to do. But he'd only been a little kid then.

This time it was different. He was a different person. So what if he blocked in front of these people? That didn't make him wrong or bad. Why should he even care about them? Matt had already learned from Archie that there were more important things to care about than whether people liked you. You had to be okay yourself, with how you were and what you did, or you'd never properly grow up.

The days dragged on. Neither Matt nor Susan had mentioned telescopes since the heart incident. The pancake breakfasts stopped too. In spite of his best efforts to avoid her, Susan caught Matt alone one morning and quietly explained that none of the girls felt up to extra cooking because of the Hero project as well as the end of year tests and exams. 'Along with other problems,' she added.

Her eyes were troubled as she looked at him. 'Are you okay?' she asked.

'Sure!' he answered, avoiding her gaze. "Fine,

thanks. Gotta go. See ya.'

He walked away. She wouldn't want to hang out with him anymore, he knew. The word had definitely got round the school about his pacifist hero. Some white feathers appeared on his desk and he heard a couple of ten year old boys chanting a really stupid rhyme about 'Yellow Belly and City Fellow' which they pronounced yeller and feller. Matt could tell they felt embarrassed when he gave them a careless thumbs up sign. He wondered who'd put them up to it. Not that any of them would have a clue what pacifism really was.

Ryan and Paul went on doing dumb things like shoving him when they could get away with it and playing the meanest rugby they could. They always stopped talking whenever he appeared and went together down to the river during breaks while the Year Eight girls hung around in a threesome. That left Matt mostly on his own, in school as well as out of it.

He spent his free time with the younger kids,

showing them more skateboard tricks, even holding the end of the skipping rope for the little girls. Just as well his friends back home couldn't see him, he thought. Faking being okay kept him going, although it wasn't like he had much choice.

Yet deep down Matt knew it was phony bravado and he wondered when he'd learned to be such a liar. Because the mean stuff did hurt, if he let himself think about it.

He was more worried lately since he'd heard that Nan and Grandpa had planned a weekend trip to see Mum. She was doing well and the baby had settled apparently. She'd written in her last email how much she was looking forward to seeing him and hearing about his new friends.

'New friends!' That was a joke. It would be great to see her but she might see right through his 'everything's fine' act.

Matt also knew how protective Mum could be over his stutter. In his emails, he'd tried to explain about Nan giving him special coaching and that she wasn't to worry about all that any more. But telling Mum not to worry was like telling the wind not to blow. She latched on to worries like a dog to a bone, telling him not to worry in a voice so tight and strangled you could hardly understand her. Yes, Mum could be a problem.

He felt disloyal even thinking such things and looked again at the crazy card that Dad had sent, wishing him well with his exams and his project. Maybe it was time for another session with the cows.

Chapter 8

Mum looked great, Matt thought later, although she did look funny with her big round belly. It had grown so much since he'd seen her last. Once she'd showed him where to put his hand to feel his little brother kicking, it was quite cool. He could feel those tiny feet whacking away at the tightly-stretched skin and imagined a little person in there. They'd all seen the picture of the baby sleeping upside down with his thumb in his mouth and there was no doubt he was a boy.

Mum's eyes were bright and she looked relaxed and happy. It was really good to see her. Luckily with everyone talking at once, there weren't too many questions about school.

Nan and Grandpa kept telling her Matt was a real help around the place and he enjoyed hearing all the extra bits and pieces about Dad and his work. Yet it was as though as soon as he saw Mum, a part of himself slammed shut with a padlock and a No Entry sign. Matt found he couldn't talk to her about his speech.

'Nothing to worry about,' he said when she asked him, uneasily aware that he might sound distant and cold. He saw the anxious eyes she turned on Nan and Grandpa but shook his head, even when she pressed him. 'No stress, Mum, remember?'

It made him feel mean, shutting her out like this but he couldn't open that padlock for anyone. Archie's story was intact in there and Matt needed it to stay that way. Nobody, absolutely nobody was going to tramp around on his careful preparation with their advice and ill-concealed panic. Especially because Matt knew that behind some offers of help would be people's secret fear that he'd mess up. Right now, he didn't need that.

He was managing to hold his world together and intended to keep it that way.

It was the anonymous letters that finally tipped that world upside down.

Matt found the letters when he collected the post as usual on the way home from school. There were two and both were addressed to him. Neither had a return address and Matt had a bad feeling as he sat down on the porch steps to read them.

Both had been written on computers and contained roughly the same content. They addressed him by his full name, Matthew Turner, and informed him in different ways that the school book project he was lucky enough to be involved in was being funded by a donation from a prominent local hero who had chosen to remain anonymous. However, Matt should know that by writing about a notorious traitor, he was behaving in a despicable way.

Archie Baxter's cowardly activities were not only insulting to the true heroes being honoured in this community but also to this generous benefactor, one letter fumed.

The first letter demanded he withdraw his story and the second recommended he immediately substitute something on another family member. Both ended with thinly-veiled threats implying that he might regret not following this advice. Neither letter was signed.

Matt found his hands trembling as he finished reading the second one. He felt sure that these were not from kids but from adults and that was mega scary. He slumped back against the steps and closed his eyes.

It wasn't until he felt the touch on his shoulder that Matt realised someone had come up beside him. Opening his eyes and seeing Nan, he wordlessly handed her the letters, hardly caring about the tear that slid down his cheek. She scanned the pages swiftly then hauled him to his feet and hugged him.

'Kitchen,' she commanded. 'Cup of tea.' This was always Nan's remedy.

'Talk to me,' she demanded a few moments later as she put a steaming mug in front of him.

Matt muttered something about mean stuff happening at school but she stopped him. 'These are not letters from kids,' she said firmly. 'But tell me anyway, what's been going on at school?'

Matt told her briefly, leaving out the part about his blocking. She knew that now anyway.

'And for some reason you felt you couldn't tell us?' She glared at him, hands on hips.

Matt repeated his promise to Mum about not worrying them. It sounded a bit lame and Nan obviously thought so too. 'Stubborn,' she sniffed, 'Stubborn and independent, just like your father!'

She sat down opposite him, sipped her tea and patted his hand. 'You're very like him, and by the way, that's not all bad! These letters though, they're particularly nasty. Any idea who's behind them?'

Matt said he didn't know but explained about someone making the contents and index pages for the Heroes book and how the trouble at school had started after that.

'But why now?' he asked. 'Grandpa said no one ever bothered him about Archie. It's old history, a hundred years ago. I don't understand?'

Nan re-read the letters and nodded. Then she seemed to come to a decision. 'Finish your tea and let's go for a drive,' she said. 'I need to tell you a story and I don't want us to be interrupted. It's a story that might help us make sense of these nasty threats.'

They headed down the road to a picnic spot beside the river and sat at one of the rough wooden tables. It was cool under the trees and the dark water swirled silently alongside. A couple of ducks waddled up, hoping for food. The drake tipped his shining green head sideways and stared at Matt, who could only stare back blankly. He still felt scared and couldn't figure how hearing some story could help. Heck, he was only a kid and these threats were from someone who seemed to know all about him.

'What I'm going to tell you concerns two people; one who's now dead, and old Cedric. Apart from us, it goes no further,' his grandmother said. 'Promise?'

Matt swiveled angrily away from the ducks. He'd already had more than enough of hearing about old Cedric but after one look at Nan's face, he promised.

'I wish you didn't have to hear this story but I think it'll help. You're not a child, Matt.'

This didn't sound too good either, but the pain in Nan's voice effectively silenced Matt's protests. He settled down and prepared to listen.

'It starts with Grandpa's mother, my mother-in-law. She was called Sylvia, an only child. Her parents were the first owners of our farm and were quite elderly when she was born. She was a shy child apparently, with a bad stutter.'

Matt looked up, astonished.

'Yes. Although there was no sign of it when I met her. Anyway, Cedric was eight years older than her and the most talked-about boy for miles around. The local kids were a bit wary of him apparently but looked up to him too. He was good looking and confident, especially after he came back from the war in 1944, wounded and already a war hero.'

'Yeah, Grandpa told me.'

'Not surprisingly, people made a huge fuss of him and next thing, a wedding's being planned between him and a young society woman from the city who'd been working in the valley as a land girl. Cedric's 21 and she's 20 and it's a match made in heaven. Only there's something about him that nobody knows.' Nan stopped, her eyes troubled.

'He's already married?' Matt hazarded a guess. 'He's a criminal?' he added hopefully.

'One evening before the wedding, he was out drinking with a few of his mates,' Nan went on as though he hadn't spoken. 'Driving home on his own, weaving all over the road, he knocked Sylvia off her bike. She was coming home after a music lesson. She wasn't badly hurt, just a bit stunned. After a bit of drunken apologising, Cedric grabbed her, held her down and – well, he virtually raped her.' Nan flushed as Matt gaped at her.

'Sylvia was only 13,' she added bluntly.

She took a deep breath. 'He was so drunk that – well, he couldn't and she managed to shove him off. Then Cedric sneered at her and said not to worry, he'd had much younger girls than her in the war, and she should take it as a compliment. Then he sobered up a bit and realised what he'd said.

After that, he lost his temper and threatened to hunt her down and really hurt her if she ever told anyone what had just happened and what he'd said. He'd claim she was chasing him, thrown herself at him. No one would believe a thirteen year old 'conchie' kid with a stupid stutter anyway, he said. So he got away with it. His wedding photos appeared in the paper and he went on being everyone's favourite hero.'

Matt was shocked. 'But surely Sylvia told someone, her parents? They'd have believed her.'

'No, she didn't tell anyone. Believe it or not, she kept it quiet her whole life, until she told me.'

'So - Grandpa?'

Nan shook her head. 'Pete doesn't know. Not even Sylvia's own husband knew and she couldn't have told her parents, from what she told me about them. Perhaps Cedric was right; no one would have believed her.'

She sighed. 'We'd always got on well, Sylvia and I. After her husband died, she came to live with us. I liked listening to her stories and one day, it just came out. She was so upset afterwards; she made me swear I would never tell Pete or your father. I've kept my promise but she didn't include you and I feel you need to know.'

Matt said nothing for a long while, trying to digest the unpalatable story. 'But why?'

'I'm getting to that, just be patient, Matt. Sylvia avoided ever speaking to Cedric again. She left the district as soon as she could after leaving school, trained as a dental nurse and married soon afterwards. When her parents died, they left her the farm. That's when she came back here. Grandpa was just a toddler.'

Matt tried unsuccessfully to imagine his grandfather as an infant but couldn't get past the bald head. 'So what happened?'

'As luck would have it, not long after they'd settled in, Cedric recognised her at an A. and P. Show, although they'd both changed a lot. It was a shock for both of them, Sylvia said.'

'What d'you mean?'

'Sylvia had grown up, she'd lost her stutter, was a confident woman. She'd worked hard to forget what had happened that night, had a fine husband, a baby, they were doing well. But not Cedric.'

'What about him?' Matt asked.

'He'd lost some of his cockiness, Sylvia said. He

seemed so different that when he begged to speak with her, she agreed. Cedric had been drinking, it turned out and was very talkative. Sylvia soon found out that he also had a son and his wife had left him three years before.'

'The kid was Freyberg? I saw him in the truck at school. He's so old. This is really weird.'

'Yes, you probably think old people like us were never young. Anyway, Cedric blustered on about how his wife didn't understand him and was a bad influence on the boy. Sylvia was disgusted and got away as soon as she could.'

'Yuck.'

'She couldn't help feeling sorry for his wife, although she'd hardly known her.'

'Pretty awful, to leave your kid behind.' Matt said, trying to cover his discomfort.

'That's what I said when Sylvia told me. She said there was a strong suspicion that Cedric was violent at home. Men often came back from the war with their nerves in tatters from what they'd done and seen, but people turned a blind eye. There wasn't the support for families back then, like there is today.'

'Anyway, after his wife left, Cedric employed married couples as sharemilkers so they could they help look after Freyberg.' She shook her head sadly.

'It's a long story, as I said, but here's the part that might make sense of those letters, Matt. After she got back, Sylvia began to hear about Cedric's activities in the local RSA and other clubs. It turned out he was very popular as a speaker about the war. He was particularly vicious about conscientious objectors, the 'cowards and traitors' and good at attacking their families. Some people loved it, especially those who'd lost someone in the war.'

'They never bothered to find out what pacifists were really on about,' Matt muttered.

'Yes, or if they knew, they kept quiet. Cedric was written up in the local newspaper and then it was rumored he'd be interviewed soon on the radio. That's when Sylvia arranged to meet him privately. She demanded that Cedric never again mention her family or the Baxters in his talks or she'd go to the RSA and the newspapers with the story of his abuse of young girls. She'd written down what had happened that night in 1945 along with her demand, and insisted that Cedric sign a copy. Cedric was furious and made a huge fuss but soon shut up when Sylvia mentioned another similar complaint that she'd got from a friend working in Army records.'

'How did she get it?' Matt asked.

'She hadn't, it was just a lucky guess,' Nan smiled grimly. 'She figured there would have been at least one and took a risk. Cedric was obviously guilty enough not to challenge her and, eventually, did sign and it was never mentioned again between them. Cedric kept his word and so did Sylvia, until it slipped out just that once to me.' Nan sighed.

'She was brave,' Matt said. 'I'm glad she got some sort of justice, but it's all so long ago. What's it got to do with me?'

'I'm telling you this, Matt, because I'm almost certain both your letters came from Freyberg. He's an odd fellow, socially awkward but he reads a lot. The formal language in the letters sounds exactly like the way he talks, even though he's tried to make them different.'

Matt shook his head stubbornly. 'I still don't get it!'

'Freyberg runs the Senior Net Computer Club. A while back I felt it might be good for him – and some of us seniors around here – so I helped him set it up. Now people know how skilled he is with computers.'

'So he did the Index, and it was Cedric who put up the money for the book. It's obvious, I should have guessed.' Matt groaned.

'The two of them were probably looking forward to reading the list of heroes and seeing who'd been chosen. After all, they've both lived here all their lives,' Nan mused.

'And then they see me writing about Archie Baxter,' Matt added.

'Yes, no doubt it stirred up the old war horse and got him snorting about pacifism again, saying his usual nasty things. Even if he didn't include us in his ranting, Freyberg would have realised that you and Pete were from a 'conchie' family, and decided to spread it around the RSA club. He probably got so excited by the reaction he got he decided to write those silly letters.'

'To support his dad. Oh, this is awful.' Matt buried his head in his hands. 'What can I do? I won't withdraw my story, no way! But those threats – '

'I'm sure that's all they are, Matt. I really don't think you need to worry about them, nasty as they are. Freyberg's always lived in the shadow of his father and never grown up. Writing those letters is probably the biggest thing he's ever done on his own. I feel certain Cedric doesn't know about them and I hope he wouldn't agree with them. He's not a bad man and his life hasn't been easy.'

She looked directly at him. 'I've great

confidence in you, Matt. All I can suggest is that you think about this. I'm sure it's the back story to those letters. Wait and see what feels right for you to do. When you decide, if you need any help, just ask. I'll say nothing to Pete, and trust that you won't either.'

Confidence in him? Matt had absolutely no idea what to do next! With the letters burning a hole in his pocket, he let off steam by hurling stones into the river while Nan watched quietly. When he was done, they drove home in silence.

'Can I photocopy the letters on your printer?' Matt asked, as Nan parked the car. He placed the originals and his copies carefully under some clothes at the back of a drawer and went to mow the lawns, hardly caring whether they needed it or not.

The noise of the mower drowned out the chaos of his thoughts as he walked slowly up and down.

Chapter 9

Matt's fears about the letters rapidly turned into anger but he couldn't decide what to do. His first reaction had been to track down Freyberg and ask why a grown man would write such mean letters, letters that he didn't have the guts to sign. He didn't much care what Freyberg thought about him. He just wanted the man to own up and mind his own business.

That was until he'd had a chance to study him at the local petrol station.

Matt had been in the back of Nan's car, because the front passenger seat was loaded with trays of sausage rolls his grandmother was taking to some event or other. As Nan filled the car, he was able to watch unseen when the son of the legendary soldier parked his car alongside and spoke to her.

With dismay, Matt watched Freyberg shuffle around to the petrol pump on his side. The man was short and stooped with neatly-combed graying hair cut very short. Although the day was warm, he had an old-fashioned anorak zipped tightly up to his chin and a woollen scarf tied round his neck. Matt couldn't help noticing how he talked in staccato bursts like he was saying sentences learned by heart.

As he spoke, he stared through thick glasses at the ground somewhere near Nan's feet, his head twisted to one side as though he'd never looked directly at anything in his life. There was definitely something a bit strange about him.

Freyberg didn't look like someone you could appeal to. After that brief glimpse, Matt didn't even have the heart to try. The guy was a lost cause. So that left Matt with – what? He still had no idea.

There was also the speech part of the project nagging away at him. Matt knew he could no longer avoid it, now the written story was out of the way.

Reluctantly he started practising in the ways that Nan had shown him. She'd given him plenty of practical ideas, how to stand steadily and breathe easily to help his voice and stomach relax; how to move his eyes freely rather than stare; how to use small notes with a few key words rather than read his story. He'd even learned that faking confidence was okay, people often did it.

Matt didn't bother mentioning he was already doing it at school anyway and when he tried it in front of the cows, they didn't seem to care. He'd already been practicing his voice exercises with them for quite a while.

Nan suggested he also act out being Archie, just to get the feel of him so Matt tried that too.

As the days passed, he began to like that there were unknown parts to himself to discover.

He knew he was changing. Something new was coming alive in him.

Matt was starting to feel certain that once people learned about Archie, their resistance to pacifism would go. How could they not respect someone who had been so decent and brave? He knew it was up to him to tell Archie's story as well as he could and that kept him going, in spite of his fears and his unreliable voice, in spite of everything.

At school, he didn't mind so much spending time with little kids any more, it felt like a sort of family. Until now, he'd always hung around with boys of his own age. Once Mrs. Foster had called him the Pied Piper because of the trail of small children behind him in the playground. They showed him knucklebones and marble games, which Matt had never played before.

He'd caught Susan watching him with the kids one day, a slight smile on her face, but looked away. He daren't risk dropping his guard with her. If she made fun of him, he didn't know if he could bear it.

Things were already bad enough with the others.

Along with being cold-shouldered and occasionally 'accidentally' roughed up by Ryan and Paul, Matt was getting some outright hostility from Shelley now, especially when Paul was with her, which was more often than not these days. The guy was obviously crazy about her. In class when the two exchanged notes and Paul looked away reddening, Matt would wonder if he was the butt of a new joke.

Shelley had a talent for sarcasm and mimicry and also unerring timing. Whenever he came across Shelley and him, Matt would hear her repeating his stuttered words to Paul with mocking emphasis, while the lovesick idiot looked on admiringly.

Matt hated hearing himself mimicked so cruelly but would concentrate hard on his breathing, pretend not to hear and ignore the unspoken battle raging between them.

These days he often felt tired and occasionally plain miserable. Yet although he sometimes longed to pretend to be sick and hide in his room at the farm, he refused to give in. He read and reread Archie's words that 'people are greater than they seem to be', and made himself keep going. The only problem was that thinking of Archie always brought him back to the letters.

Later when Matt looked back at that time, he could see he'd cloaked his anger in politeness. It was a trick that could fool some people but worst of all, he'd deceived himself.

It needed someone who'd used the same trick to see through it.

Chapter 10

'Excuse me,' he said automatically to Susan without looking at her, as she barred his way late one afternoon. Apart from them, the school was empty and he was trying to collect his bag from the outside hooks to go home.

'No,' she said, glaring at him, arms folded. 'There's no excuse for what you're doing and I can't stand it anymore.'

Matt stared at her, not understanding. 'I said, excuse m-me!' He tried to push past her and grab his bag but she blocked him again.

'S-susan, I want my bag.' Matt was furious

now. 'P-please.'

'Oh, sooo polite, but you don't fool me.'

'I want my bloody bag,' he yelled.

'That's better. Fight me for it!' she retorted. Hands on hips, she challenged him, eyes blazing. Matt had never seen her like this.

'Fight me or talk to me, it's your choice. Or no bag.'

He couldn't hit her, Matt knew that. He'd never hit anyone, let alone a girl, she probably counted on it.

'Talk about what?' he yelled back. There was no one around to hear them.

'Whatever's eating you and turning you into such a poisonous pain in the neck.'

'Me?' Matt was livid. 'ME! It's everyone else in this school that's poisonous. I can't wait to get out of here.'

'Oh, so you're human after all. I was starting to think you'd got bullet-proof clothing under your tee-shirts.'

Matt reached past her and angrily grabbed his bag. He smelled the clean fresh scent of her and was painfully reminded of their star gazing.

'Go on then. You've got your bag, so go! Or do you want to talk?'

'What d'you mean, bullet-proof clothing?' Matt hesitated.

Susan pushed past him and made for the swings. It had been their favourite place to talk and instinctively he followed her. She chose one of the larger ones and slowly pushed off.

'I've watched you. There's been lots of mean stuff aimed at you and you're completely ignoring it. It's as though it's not happening. Don't you care?'

'Of course I care!' Matt swung angrily beside her. 'What am I supposed to do? I'm on my own here. In case you haven't noticed, Ryan and Paul aren't the only ones being shitty.'

'Maybe they're afraid of you. No one over eight years old can get near you anymore!' Susan retorted.

'That's dumb,' Matt snapped back.

'Okay, so they mouthed off about Archie Baxter, said some stupid things. They know nothing about pacifism. So what? Ryan's been jealous of you ever since you arrived, I suppose you know that?'

Matt stared at her.

'Hey, you're the city kid. Under that tough guy act, he and Paul are scared stiff of leaving here for college with hundreds of others. They've got used to being the big boys around here.'

'Serves them right!' Matt was still defensive and angry. 'I don't care about them anyway. They're doing their own thing, let them!'

'Any idea what that is?'

'Huh?' Matt was puzzled.

'Their own thing? I don't suppose it occurred to you that other people might have troubles apart from you?' Susan stopped swinging and glared at him again. 'Ryan's family have big money problems, they might lose their farm. It's been in their family for a hundred years, the whole district's upset about it. Everyone's trying to help, almost everyone,' she added meaningfully.

Matt could think of nothing to say. Money problems? Was that why they stopped talking when he appeared? 'Idiot,' he thought. 'Dumb, dumb and dumber for thinking the world revolves around you.'

'But Shelley and Paul?' he ventured aloud.

'Yeah, Shelley, I know she can be mean. You're not her first target, believe me. Has it occurred to you why she won't leave you alone?'

Matt shook his head.

'She likes you, dumbo. She's using poor old Paul to try and make you jealous.'

This was too much. Matt shook his head slowly, he felt as though he'd been hit with a brick. Shelley? She liked him?

'My blocking, she's been so awful about it –'

'Yeah, like I said, she can be mean. She's not used to being ignored, that's why she's doing it.'

'But I never meant to -,' he began helplessly.

'Hey, you never even noticed her or if you did,

you looked uneasy. Girls pick up on these things.'

Susan swung on serenely, kicking her legs like a two year old.

'Why are you –' Once again, Matt couldn't finish.

'Why am I telling you this? Why am I bothering? Because I can spot a sham a mile off, especially one who's faking that they're okay by being bullet-proof and super-perfect polite.'

She ignored his protests and went on.

'I know because I've done it too. I've made myself sick trying to deal with bad stuff on my own and pretending to be cool and okay. No one should have to do it, I know that now. It's too hard and it messes you up.'

She slowed her swinging until she sat silently beside him. So much was left unsaid between them but Matt felt too full and choked up to say anything.

They got off the swings and Matt waited silently while Susan collected her bike. At the gate, they paused.

'Hey, Susan, thanks.'

She ducked her head, smiling.

'I'll lend you my bullet-proof vests any time,' he added, grinning.

'I thought I'd need one today, but you're not so scary after all!' she shot back.

'See you tomorrow!'

'See ya!' she said, smiling. 'Kick a few rocks on the way home. It works for me.'

Chapter 11

Maybe it was kicking the rocks or maybe it was Susan's unexpected support, but Matt now knew what to do about the letters. It needed some careful planning and took him ages, but he did it.

He also faced up to the fact that in spite of his best efforts, he was just imitating Archie Baxter and it was half killing him. Heck, the guy was incredible, he really didn't care what other people thought of him, while Matt just pretended not to. Even admitting that much made him feel better.

He needed to put things straight with Shelley and chose a time when Paul wasn't with her. She was sitting on a bench in the sunshine re-arranging her long hair when he sat down beside her.

'I've been thinking, maybe we've misunderstood each other,' he began conversationally. 'Maybe we've got the same problem.'

Shelley's pale eyes widened. 'Mind your own business!' she snapped. 'I don't have a problem, although y-you d-do,' she ended cruelly.

'When I block, it's because I've let myself care what people think of me,' Matt's tone stayed calm although rage was shimmering inside him. 'You care too, or you wouldn't have to do what you did just now.'

'That's where you're wrong. I don't care! I don't care what anyone thinks, especially y-you, M-matt T-turner,' she sneered.

Matt stood up. 'D'you know, you look quite ugly when you're throwing a tantrum. It's a shame,' he observed in surprise and walked away. It was true. Shelley was pretty and yet she looked awful in that moment.

Maybe vanity will make her clean up her act, he thought. Well, at least he'd tried. It hadn't been very subtle, but it might give her something else to obsess about.

There was nothing he could think of to say to Ryan and Paul; he was too angry. Instead, during rugby practice he threw himself into the game like a maniac, hurling the ball at them as if it was a live grenade. The other two quickly caught onto his mood and the three of them fought a fast and furious battle on the field, striving to outdo the other. Not once did they manage to trip him or knock him off balance.

When the whistle blew they collapsed on the sideline, streaming with sweat and glared at each other.

'Whew,' puffed Ryan. 'I wouldn't like to meet you on a dark night.'

'At least you'd know I wouldn't be carrying a gun,' Matt snapped back. 'My pacifist family and all that! Remember?'

'Yeah,' Ryan looked away.

'What's it to you, what my family does? Or what I do, or Susan for that matter. You don't own her!'

'Get lost!' snarled Ryan, his face reddening. .

Matt stared at him defiantly then turned to Paul who shrugged and looked away.

'Okay, so we've shoved you around a bit; you didn't seem to care.'

'Fat lot you know,' Matt growled. The whistle blew for the second half and they ran back onto the field, but something between them had changed.

After this, Matt's life at school became marginally easier. Shelley ignored him completely and that was a relief. She'd also dismissed Paul from her company and the poor guy was always looking for someone to toss a ball with. Matt obliged once but continued to spend a lot of his time with the little kids. Ryan just avoided him.

The days flew by until all Year Eight exams and tests were finished and only the detested speech event was left.

Finally, inevitably, the dreaded evening arrived. Matt waited in the kitchen, knowing that in five minutes it would be time to leave for the school. He felt there was nothing more he could do in the way of preparation.

He carefully re-arranged his five cue cards, cut small to fit neatly into his hand and numbered in the top right corner. 'Just like the politicians use,' Nan had said. The cards with their key prompt words gave Matt something to hold, as well as a feeling of security.

His father's laugh rang out loudly over the excited chatter of voices in the dining room. It had been awesome, Dad turning up the way he did. It was supposed to be a surprise but Mum had been unable to resist telling Matt he was coming back from Hong Kong for a few days.

She had a specialist medical appointment about the baby that Dad needed to be there for, and he'd managed to fit in an overnight trip to see Matt and his own parents. Mum made sure his visit was timed for the end of term evening and in his turn, Matt promised to act surprised. It wasn't hard; Dad had been away so long.

When he'd walked in, Nan and Grandpa had nearly jumped out of their skins. Matt had never seen them so shaken.

'Ken! Oh, Ken!' Nan kept saying, wiping her eyes with her apron while Grandpa stood by, tugging his ear and looking stunned. Matt thought Dad might break some of his own ribs, he hugged him so hard. It was brilliant to see him, so much better than Skype.

He was loaded down with presents from Hong Kong. They planned to open them tomorrow as an early Christmas, in case Dad didn't make it back for the real event. Even if he missed it by a day or so, they were guaranteed at least ten weeks together, he told Matt. 'It'll soon be over.'

'By tomorrow, all this will be over too,' Matt told himself. 'I just have to tell everyone a real hero's story.'

At that moment, his father came into the kitchen. A flicker of anxiety crossed his face as his eyes rested on the cards 'Everything okay, Matt?' he asked. Matt guessed he was remembering all those other times. His own response was more cheerful than he felt.

'All okay,' he said. 'Just want to keep quiet now, so I don't forget my words.' And so it was that their family arrived at the school hall that evening in almost total silence. Grandpa drove with the concentration of a rally driver, a frown on his face and his jaw set. He'd been made to wear his best clothes and looked stiff and uncomfortable.

Dad sat quietly beside him, shooting occasional sympathetic glances into the back seat, where Matt sat beside Nan. She'd also dressed up for the occasion but seemed relaxed.

Matt balanced the enormous cake she'd made for supper on his knee, the smell of the chocolate peppermint icing making him feel slightly sick.

'Go well, Matt!' his grandfather said at last,

pulling into a parking space. 'See you at suppertime.' His father squeezed his shoulder and gave him a wink while Nan offered a warm smile as they entered the hall. The three adults were soon absorbed into the noisy crowd.

As Matt made his way towards the stage at the other end of the room, he sensed several men studying him. Their eyes were appraising and he looked away. A small group of women stopped chattering and watched curiously as he pushed past the tightly-packed rows of chairs and benches. 'So that's the Turner boy,' he heard one of them say.

Blindly, Matt shoved his way forward to join the other kids on stage. Who were these people? Why couldn't they leave him alone! For a moment, angry panic threatened to swamp him and then he remembered Archie's voice, not his real voice of course but the voice that Matt had given him. 'Not much longer now.' The fear subsided and he felt strangely calm.

As he moved into the semi-darkness behind the

heavy blue stage curtains, the first person he saw was Ryan, slumped in a chair with his head in his hands, while Paul paced up and down, his hair standing on end and his eyes wild. 'Shit, shit, shit,' Matt heard him muttering. 'I can't remember a word.'

To Matt's surprise, they both greeted him with relief. 'This has got to be the worst part of the year,' Ryan moaned. 'Don't you reckon?'

'Yup.' Matt wasn't lying. He could see the three Year Eight girls clustered together in one nervous group, fussing over each other's hair.

Paul came over to him. 'Wouldn't mind learning some of those skateboard stunts this weekend, if you're still around and speaking to me. Once this nightmare's over. Oh no, where are my notes? My old man'll kill me if I get any dates wrong.' He grabbed at some large untidy pages and resumed his frantic pacing while Matt sat down on a chair near Ryan and let out a sigh.

Ryan looked up. 'I hate doing this more than anything.'

'Soon be over,' Matt offered. 'Imagine the audience naked, then they don't seem so scary.'

Ryan snorted with laughter and blew his nose. 'Good one! I'll try it.'

Matt could see he was sweating and really nervous. Maybe the guy wasn't so tough. It would be hard to lose your home and farm.

Mrs. Foster called all the kids to line up and Matt found himself standing beside Susan. 'Good luck,' they both whispered at the same time. 'I've missed our star gazing,' she said softly.

'Me too.' Matt flashed her a happy grin as they stepped out from behind the curtain onto the stage. They sat awkwardly in their curved rows of chairs, blinking into the lights focused on the stage.

First came votes of thanks to practically everyone in the district, as far as Matt could tell. Next Mr. Foster explained how he'd come up with this project to honour the community's own heroes who had passed on and an anonymous gift had paid for it.

At last Mrs. Foster uncovered the book itself and lifted it up to show everyone. As she turned it from side to side, displaying its pages, there was a spontaneous rush of applause and Matt found himself clapping as well.

The book was impressive, really big and bound in what looked like leather with gilt lettering. It looked good enough to go in a library or even an art gallery, Matt thought.

Senior Net members were thanked for their help, others for the book introduction and adding in the photos of the kids with their stories and soon there was nothing left to do but hear the six speeches.

Year Eight had drawn lots for speaking positions and Shelley went first, telling about a RNZAF helicopter pilot who served in Vietnam. She sat down to a generous round of applause.

Bronwyn's hero was a surprise. She'd chosen an early surveyor who lived off his wits and the land as he'd travelled all over the South Island with a couple of Māori guides, creating his maps. Matt particularly liked the bit about him entertaining his companions and the local birds with his harmonica.

Paul was next. He delivered his speech at breakneck speed, reading from his notes in a frantic monotone and ending with an audible gasp of relief. The audience cheered him good-naturedly and someone yelled out, 'I vote for Paul as our next auctioneer for the stock yards!' to general laughter.

Then it was Matt's turn to stand and go forward. He stood looking out at the upturned faces. For a moment, terror seized him and then an image of the cows placidly chewing and patiently listening flashed into his mind. He could do this. Just as Nan had taught him, he counted backwards from five and then began.

Chapter 12

Matt's voice rang out clearly in the hall. 'Come with me to the battle grounds in Europe. In a muddy wasteland somewhere, a man hangs tied to a post. Is he dead? He wears no uniform and ...'

As Matt led his audience through his introduction, there was a sudden hush and he knew that he had them. The trick had worked. All shuffling ceased and he felt the attention of the whole room trained on him.

Without hesitation, he took them through the horrors inflicted on this unknown man and the insights that made him able to endure them.

After such cruelties, his inglorious home-coming seemed almost tame. Yet when Matt told them how, returning to that unnamed land, this damaged hero was denied the right to vote for ten years, something that no other country did, many looked outraged.

When they further heard how he and his family continued to be ostracized and ridiculed, some shook their heads in distress.

Matt paused then, and when the room was quiet said, 'For those of you who haven't already guessed, my hero is Archie Baxter, World War One pacifist, and his home country is New Zealand.'

Ignoring the gasps of shock and surprise, he went swiftly on, aware of his father and grandparents in the front row. 'Although we're only distantly related to those Baxters, like many in my family, I've had a taste of what he went through. A very small taste, but a warning, all the same of how some people believe anyone who won't fight is a coward.' The taboo topic was out in the open at last and seemed to hang in the air. Matt could almost feel the suspense. He left it hanging there, so much unspoken but understood, and moved confidently towards the end of his story.

The conclusion surprised most people, as he'd known it would. Nan's advice had been brilliant.

Instead of stopping at Archie's death, Matt went on to tell his audience that anti-militarist convictions were very much alive in one country where three generations of kids already had grown up safely in a culture where it's normal, not weird, to have no military forces. 'It's a nation where no one gets offered a career in learning to fight other people, often called peace keeping,' he said.

He'd explained how Costa Rica in Central America had permanently abolished its army in 1949. Since then, in spite of military coups and invasions by the super powers in countries to the north and to the south, no nation was willing to be seen as so cowardly that they would invade an unarmed state.

No resource-hungry nation could whip up a military rebellion in a country where there were no armed forces.

Costa Rica's decision had been a bold and courageous move and had worked for them.

'It's not perfect, far from it, but what country is? Today Costa Rica's often listed as the world's happiest and greenest country with the most sustainable environment,' he told them. 'They spend less than one percent of their wealth on public security and police, where some other countries spend twenty percent or more. That means heaps more money for education and health. In a world where literacy levels are falling fast, Costa Rica's literacy is over 90 percent and rising. Forty per cent of working Kiwis struggle with literacy today. Think about that!'

In a school, it was the perfect ending. Nan had been right. The response was more than polite; stamps of approval and a cheer accompanied the applause and Matt flushed with pleasure as he made his way back to his seat.

Ryan's speech followed and was a straight-forward account of his relative's rise to the rank of Colonel in the Second World War. He hadn't been joking about the family calling him Horrible Henry apparently and several chuckles could be heard from the hall. Ryan got through it well enough and, Matt had to admit, it was a well-researched story.

The evening ended with Susan speaking about a woman astronomer and cosmologist, celebrated today for her discoveries in the face of discrimination and bias. She was clapped at almost every anecdote, with Matt clapping the loudest.

When their obligatory class photo was taken a few minutes later, Ryan and Paul moved apart so Matt could stand between them. It felt okay being with them again.

During supper afterwards, quite a few kids said they thought Archie sounded really cool. Several fathers congratulated him and promised to tell him about the trouble his father got into at school, knowing full well that Dad was within earshot, a huge smile on his face.

Matt had heard his father being greeted on all sides. 'Ken, it's great to see you. How did you manage to produce this young firebrand?'

Dad slung his arm around Matt's shoulders and held him close. 'He takes after me, of course,' he joked. 'Although luckily not in his speaking skills!'

'Yeah, we remember!'

'That was great, Matt,' his father added quietly as the others moved away. 'It was time to tell Archie's story here. You've done something I could never do. You may have been nervous, but it didn't show. I'm so proud of you and Mum will be too, I know it.'

'I really miss her!'

Dad squeezed his shoulder. 'Me too. Not long now.'

Those words again. Then they both heard Matt's name called. It was Mr. Foster, still presiding over the book and Dad let him go.

'Well done, Matt, that was an excellent story,' Mr. Foster beamed at him. 'You had us all on the edge of our seats, even though Mrs. Foster and I'd been lucky enough to skim read the book already. We're very impressed with your writing, Matt. You make history come alive.'

'We'd like to put your tale into our series of stories leading up to New Zealand's nuclear free stand,' Mrs. Foster added. 'With your permission, of course. We both feel that pacifists should stand alongside people like Nelson Mandela, Martin Luther King and others.'

Mr. Foster coughed, embarrassed. 'It's not a topic I knew much about, pacifism. I'm grateful you've brought it out of the shadows, Matt. Makes a welcome change. And Costa Rica!' He sighed. 'Those literacy levels – that's very inspiring. I must find time to read about it.'

Matt could only mumble that Nan had put him onto that particular story. 'If old Cedric could hear this,' he thought to himself. 'I wonder what he'd say?'

He fingered the folded page in his pocket, a copy of what he'd written to the old soldier. It has been his good luck charm, a magic talisman in case the evening went horribly wrong.

The single page had taken hours to write. Matt had written dozens of copies until he finally said what he wanted to say in fifty words – he was proud of that. He'd personally delivered it to Cedric, along with the photocopies of the two letters.

He'd worked out the whole plan one sleepless night and said nothing about it to anyone else. It was a huge bluff on his part but he was determined to risk it.

Following Matt's phone call to him, Cedric had been waiting, upright and dignified, outside his front door. On the phone, he'd simply asked to see the old man for help with some family business and there'd been no questions. Perhaps he already guessed what it was about.

Matt arrived punctually at the agreed time, having even combed his hair, and handed over the envelope.

He watched as the pages were quickly scanned, then fiercely crumpled into a ball in the large, arthritic fists. There was a long silence as Cedric stared long and hard into the distance.

Matt began to wonder what to do next.

'Your father was a first-class shot,' the old man said gruffly at last, startling him. This wasn't the response Matt had imagined.

'I taught him to shoot first with a slug gun and then a rifle, at tin cans and then at possums. Ken always had a steady hand,' He snorted wryly at Matt's stunned expression.

'We had to keep it quiet, mind you. No guns allowed in your family! And Freyberg's fairly useless with firearms.'

Matt could think of nothing to say in return.

Brandishing his fistful of papers, the old solider grunted 'Brave lad!' and went into his house, slamming the door. Matt hadn't known what to expect, but not this. Yet those words about Dad were oddly reassuring. And who was the brave lad,

Dad or himself? He didn't know, but it would be okay, he was certain.

He'd been right. Standing listening now to the Fosters talking about Archie, he remembered the encouraging 'Stick to your guns, lad!' from old Cedric as he and Freyberg passed by in the crowd gathered around the supper table.

The note had worked. As though on a blackboard its contents appeared in his mind, a gift from his training with his grandmother.

'As her only great-grandchild, Sylvia Turner left me certain family papers. They include an agreement signed by herself and someone who is respected as a man of his word. I feel confident this man will want to observe this agreement and stop at their source the accusations in these letters.'

Okay, there'd been a few sour looks cast his way over supper. He knew that some people would be angry with him for doubting the heroics of war. But at least he'd offered an alternative. 'Hey, there's not a white feather in sight!' he told himself happily. He'd done it.

Later, loading his plate with cake for the second time, he found himself standing beside his grandfather.

'You did well!' Grandpa said, eyeing Matt thoughtfully. 'After practically giving me a heart attack when I thought you were going to talk about...' He dropped his voice, 'Old Cedric.'

'No need, Grandpa,' Matt's smile was wide. 'The message got through.'

'History's been re-written here tonight. You can't imagine the comments I've heard. You've got guts, I'll grant you that!' Grandpa seemed shocked, surprised and pleased, all at the same time.

Matt ate his way rapidly through his cake, then went looking for Nan.

He found her in the kitchen, chatting with a group of women over the inevitable cup of tea. The room was large and airy with teapots as big as buckets crowding round the sink. Trays of savouries warmed in the oven while fresh plates of scones waited for space on the supper tables.

'Here's a new recruit for the Drama Club!' one of the women cried, seeing him come in. 'That was a fine speech, Matt. I had tears in my eyes listening to you. I knew nothing about Archie Baxter and now I have to find out more. We'll be getting his book for the library.'

'You spoke very well,' another said, looking at him curiously. 'Did your grandmother share any of her secrets with you, by any chance?'

Matt winked at Nan. 'Couldn't possibly comment,' he said.

'It's all in the genes,' Nan added mysteriously.

In the car going home, Matt looked out the window at the stars, so brilliant in the clear sky. Out here, you could see heaps more of almost every constellation. It was a perfect night for his telescope.

He yawned. There'd be presents to open in the morning before Dad left. The telescope could wait until tomorrow night when Paul and Ryan were coming over with Susan.

He'd definitely go to Costa Rica one day, he decided.

Before he went, he'd find out the names of some teachers and maybe even people in the government and he'd give them a copy of Archie's book. He'd tell them about him, Archibald Baxter, a hero from a century ago and a country far away, a man whose example had inspired far more people than he could ever have imagined.

About the Author

Linda Hansen spent her early years on a dairy farm in the Bay of Plenty and lists cows and cats among her favourite animals. She writes for adults and children and was very pleased to win the *2012 Jack Lasenby Children's Writing Award* for her story 'Socks'.

For the past ten years she has also worked as a Storyteller, telling tales in schools, rest homes and in other places. She remembers what it felt like being scared in front of an audience when she first started out.

Linda wrote 'An Unexpected Hero' because she feels it is important that the 'other' story be told about what happened to many New Zealanders after the First World War began in 1914.

Teachers' Resource Kits

A comprehensive Teachers' Resource Kit for
'An Unexpected Hero'
is available as a free download from
www.createbooks.co.nz

Teachers' Resource Kits are also available from
www.createbooks.co.nz for the books:
Batjack
How to Stop Being Bullied
The Sea and Me
The Trees and Me

Other books published by
CreateBooks include:
Ivan I. Dear
How to Bully-Proof Your Child
R.I.P. Cyberbullying

www.createbooks.co.nz
info@createbooks.co.nz